One
The Lead and Collar

Rupert died when Janie was only two, so she didn't really remember anything about him.

She knew what he looked like, of course – there were lots of photos of him: on his own, or with Mum or Dad, and one she specially liked of herself as a toddler sitting on the lawn with Rupert standing beside her. She was just sorry she'd never known him.

'Mum,' Janie said one day, 'how long ago did Rupert die?'

'Oh, let's see,' her mother said. 'He died when you were two and now you're seven. So – five years ago.'

'And how old was he?'

'He was eight.'

'That's not very old for a dog, is it?' Janie said.

'Not for most dogs,' her mother said, 'but then Rupert was very big, a giant really. Great Danes don't usually live as long as smaller dogs.'

'What did he die of?'

'Kidney failure.'

'Were you and Daddy sad?'

PUFFIN BOOKS

The INVISIBLE DOG

Dick King-Smith served in the Grenadier Guards during the Second World War, and afterwards spent twenty years as a farmer in Gloucestershire, the county of his birth. Many of his stories are inspired by his farming experiences. Later he taught at a village primary school. His first book, *The Fox Busters*, was published in 1978. Since then he has written a great number of children's books, including *The Sheep-Pig* (winner of the Guardian Award and filmed as *Babe*), *Harry's Mad*, *Noah's Brother*, *The Hodgeheg*, *Martin's Mice*, *Ace*, *The Cuckoo Child* and *Harriet's Hare* (winner of the Children's Book Award in 1995). At the British Book Awards in 1991 he was voted Children's Author of the Year. He has three children, a large number of grandchildren and several great-grandchildren, and lives in a seventeenth-century cottage only a crow's-flight from the house where he was born.

Dick King-Smith

The
INVISIBLE DOG

Illustrated by Ann Kronheimer

PUFFIN

PUFFIN BOOKS

Published by the Penguin Group
Penguin Books Ltd, 80 Strand, London WC2R 0RL, England
Penguin Group (USA) Inc., 375 Hudson Street, New York, New York 10014, USA
Penguin Group (Canada), 90 Eglinton Avenue East, Suite 700, Toronto, Ontario, Canada M4P 2Y3
(a division of Pearson Penguin Canada Inc.)
Penguin Ireland, 25 St Stephen's Green, Dublin 2, Ireland (a division of Penguin Books Ltd)
Penguin Group (Australia), 250 Camberwell Road, Camberwell, Victoria 3124, Australia
(a division of Pearson Australia Group Pty Ltd)
Penguin Books India Pvt Ltd, 11 Community Centre, Panchsheel Park, New Delhi – 110 017, India
Penguin Group (NZ), 67 Apollo Drive, Rosedale, North Shore 0632, New Zealand
(a division of Pearson New Zealand Ltd)
Penguin Books (South Africa) (Pty) Ltd, 24 Sturdee Avenue, Rosebank, Johannesburg 2196, South Africa

Penguin Books Ltd, Registered Offices: 80 Strand, London WC2R 0RL, England

puffinbooks.com

First published by Viking 1995
Published in Puffin Books 1997
Published with new illustrations 2003
This edition published 2010

3

Text copyright © Fox Busters Ltd, 1995
Illustrations copyright © Ann Kronheimer, 2003
Extract from *The Queen's Nose*: text copyright © Fox Busters Ltd, 1983
illustrations copyright © Ann Kronheimer, 2005
All rights reserved

The moral right of the author and illustrator has been asserted

Set in 15/18.5pt Perpetua
Made and printed in England by Clays Ltd, St Ives plc

British Library Cataloguing in Publication Data
A CIP catalogue record for this book is available from the British Library

ISBN: 978-0-141-33237-6

www.greenpenguin.co.uk

Contents

'Terribly.'

'Is that why we've never had a dog since?'

'I suppose it is, really. We talked about getting a puppy, but somehow it seemed as though no other dog could replace Rupert, so we never did.'

'What kind of puppy would you have got?' asked Janie.

'Oh, a Great Dane again, I think. We wouldn't want any other sort of dog. But they're awfully expensive to buy and awfully expensive to keep.'

'Shall we ever have another one, d'you think?'

'I don't know, darling,' Janie's mother said. 'We'll see.'

'We'll see', Janie knew, always meant

'probably not and don't go pestering me about it or it'll be certainly not'. So she thought she'd better drop the subject.

However, the spirit of the late great Rupert must have decided otherwise, for only a few days later Janie came by chance upon something she'd never set eyes on before.

She was hunting about at the back of the garage, where her father had his workbench, looking for an oil can to oil her bike, when she saw something hanging high on a nail in a dark dusty corner.

It was a dog collar with a lead attached.

Janie climbed up on to the bench and took it down.

The collar was a very big, broad, brass-studded one with a round metal disc

attached to the buckle. She rubbed the disc clear of dust and there, scratched on the face, was the name RUPERT and, underneath, their telephone number.

Janie put the collar to her nose. It smelt of leather and dog, and just  for a moment it made her feel sad to think that this faint smell was all that was left of the creature whose great neck the collar had encircled. How many hundreds of times in his eight years of life would he have gone for a walk wearing it, with Mum or Dad holding the end of the thick plaited lead?

Janie went out of the garden gate and wandered up the lane, the loop of the lead in her left hand, the empty collar dangling. She looked down at the thick leather circlet and imagined the shape and sweep of the great neck, the Great Dane neck, within it. She saw the dog clearly in her mind's eye as it walked beside her.

Lost in a daydream, she almost bumped into Mrs Garrow, an elderly widow who lived alone in one of the cottages at the top end of the village.

'Hullo, Janie! Where are you off to then?' said the old lady with a loud laugh. Mrs Garrow's laugh sounded like nothing so much as a duck quacking.

'I'm taking my dog for a walk,' Janie
said.

'I can see that,' said Mrs Garrow, and
she put out a hand and patted the air

Want to know what some of our readers thought of this book?

'I liked the free kick that Adam scored.
Adam was my favourite'

Jude, age 7

'The best thing about this story was Adam
and James because Adam was kind'

Ryan, age 7

'I liked it when Adam and James
share the Golden Boot Trophy'

Jordan, age 10

behind the dangling collar, just where the dog's back would have been.

'Who's a good boy then?' said Mrs Garrow. 'He's looking ever so well, Janie; you must be proud of him. Make sure you keep him on the lead, mind; there's a lot of traffic in the lane these days,' and she went on her way, quacking loudly.

Some people never grow too old for games of make-believe, thought Janie. That's nice. And two can play at that.

'Heel!' she said, and she walked on, the invisible dog pacing at her side.

Two
The Name

After Janie had gone to bed that night, her parents were talking.

'I see Janie's got hold of old Rupert's collar and lead,' her father said.

'Yes,' her mother said. 'She's been carrying it around all day. It's lying beside her bed now.'

'When I arrived home from work,' her father said, 'she was so engrossed with it I don't think she even heard the car. She was walking round the lawn, dangling the collar and talking away to an imaginary animal. Every now and then she'd stop and say, 'Sit!' and then after a bit she'd say, 'Heel!' and walk on again.'

'I know. I can only think she must have a very vivid imagination to play a game like that for so long.'

'Has she been pestering you to get a puppy?'

11

'No. It would be nice though, David, wouldn't it? One day.'

'Another Great Dane?'

'Of course.'

'Oh, come off it, Sally,' Janie's father said. 'They're awfully expensive to buy and awfully expensive to keep. I mean, these days a decent Dane puppy costs over three hundred pounds.'

'You know that, do you?'

'Well . . . yes, I just happened to notice an advertisement. And as for feeding a growing pup – well, you can reckon on over six hundred pounds a year.'

'So we can't afford one?'

'No. You weren't seriously thinking of getting one?'

'No.'

'Right then.'

At breakfast next morning they both
noticed that the loop of the lead was
round Janie's left wrist as she ate, the
collar on the floor beside her.

'Do we have to have that dirty old thing
at the table?' her father asked.

'He's not a dirty old thing,' Janie said.

'He? I'm talking about the collar and
lead.'

'Oh sorry, Dad, I thought you were
talking about my dog.'

'It's a funny thing,' her mother said, 'but
Daddy and I can't actually *see* a dog.'

'You wouldn't,' said Janie. 'He's
invisible.'

'I see.'

'No you don't, Mum.'

'I mean, I hear what you're saying.
By the way, what do you feed him on?'

'Invisible food.'

'In an invisible dish?'

'Naturally.'

'Think of the money you're saving,' Janie's father said, 'never having to fork out for dog meat or biscuits. Can't cost you a penny.'

'Of course it does, Daddy. When we go shopping today, you wouldn't believe how much I shall have to spend.'

'Invisible money?'

'Of course.'

'Has he got a name, this invisible dog?' her mother asked.

'Well, no, not yet,' said Janie. 'I haven't decided.'

'Have you decided what breed he is?' her father said.

'Oh honestly, Daddy!' said Janie. 'I

should have thought that you'd have
known a Great Dane when you saw
one.'

'You could just call him Rupert,' her
mother said. 'That's what's written on his
collar, after all.'

'No,' said Janie. 'I think this dog ought
to have a different name, don't you?'

'Oh yes,' they said.

'I mean, he's quite a different colour,
isn't he?'

'Is he?' they said.

'Rupert was a fawn dog, with a black
mask,' Janie's father said.

'Whereas this one,' Janie's mother said,
'is . . . um . . . well . . . what would you
say, Janie?'

'Black with white splodges,' said Janie.

'Or white with black splodges, whichever you like to say.'

'A harlequin Great Dane!' they cried. 'Of course.'

'So he really needs a sort of black-and-white name, doesn't he?'

'Like Magpie, you mean?' said her mother.

'Or Zebra,' said her father.

'Or Panda.'

'Or Penguin.'

'Yes,' said Janie, 'but I don't like any of those names. I think I'll just call him Spotty.'

'You can't!' they cried with one voice. 'You can't call a harlequin Great Dane "Spotty". It's not dignified enough.'

'He's my dog,' said Janie, and she put

down a hand and stroked an invisible back, 'so I can call you Spotty if I want to, or Tom, Dick or Harry.'

'He liked "Harry",' said Janie's father, looking down at the collar lying on the floor. 'He wagged his tail a bit when you said "Harry".'

Janie's mother raised her eyes to heaven.

'Oh honestly, David!' she said. 'You're as bad as she is. No doubting where she gets it from.'

'Harry,' said Janie. 'I quite like that.'

'Or perhaps Henry,' said her father. 'That's a bit more dignified.'

'Henry?' said Janie. 'Henry! Yes, you're right, Daddy. He's wagging his tail like mad now. Henry it is!'

Three
The Price

All this happened towards the end of the holidays and, as the new term approached, Janie's parents began to wonder if Henry would be taken to school.

They worried at the thought of their child doing lessons or playing games or eating her lunch, always attached to the lead and collar. It was all very well to make-believe at home, but whatever would the teachers think?

They waited, a little nervously, for the first day of term.

'Got all your school things ready?' her father said at breakfast.

'Yes.'

Her mother drew a deep breath.

'You're not taking Henry, are you, darling?' she said.

'Oh honestly, Mummy!' said Janie. 'You know we're not allowed pets at school, not even a gerbil, let alone a Great Dane. But he can come in the car with us, can't he?'

'Oh. Yes. Of course.'

'And then he can go back home with

you once you've dropped Daddy off at the station.'

'All right.'

'You'll have to exercise him, Mum.'

'Take him for a walk, d'you mean?' her mother asked nervously.

'No, just let him out for a run in the garden. Mind you take his lead off or he'll trip over it. Just let him out at lunch time, that'll be enough. After all, we don't want Henry making a mess in the house. Specially an invisible mess.'

'I wonder what it would be like,' said her father thoughtfully, 'stepping in an invisible dog mess?'

When, however, her mother drove to fetch Janie at the end of the school

day, she found that she had forgotten
something. As they came out of the
playground and reached the car, parked at
the roadside, Janie looked in at the back
seat and made a little noise of
disappointment.

'Oh, Mum!' she said. 'You left Henry at home.'

Janie's mother stopped herself on the verge of saying, 'No, he's there all right, it's just that he's invisible.' From then on she was always careful, whenever she collected Janie, to have put the collar at one or other end of the back seat and the lead ready for Janie to clip on when they arrived home.

'Have you told them at school?' Janie's mum said, a few days later.

'Told who?'

'Your friends.'

'What about?'

'About Henry.'

'No. But I told our teacher,' said Janie.

'What! That we'd got a Great Dane?'

'No. Just that we might have one, one day. Another one, I mean, as well as Henry.'

'What makes you think that?'

'Well, we might, Mum, mightn't we? You never know what's going to happen.'

'I do,' her mother said, 'and we aren't. Your father wouldn't consider it.'

'How d'you know?'

'You ask him.'

So when her father came home from work that evening, Janie did.

She didn't for one moment think that he'd say yes, though she half hoped for a 'We'll see', which would mean there might be a chance, but he simply said, 'No, of course not. Can't afford it.'

'How much would a puppy cost then?'

Janie said. 'A Great Dane puppy, I mean. A harlequin Great Dane.'

Her father stopped himself on the verge of saying 'three hundred pounds'. Possibly that was a guess on the low side, he thought, and probably harlequins are more expensive than other colours, and anyway, if I say a really high price she'll forget the whole silly business.

'Five hundred pounds,' he said.

Janie looked down at the collar, dangling as usual from its lead, and patted an invisible head.

'D'you hear that, Henry?' she said. 'Just think what you must be worth.'

'You stick to Henry,' her father said.

'I could save up my pocket money,' Janie said.

'Take you about ten years.'

'Just think! I'd be seventeen,' said Janie, 'nearly eighteen, and then I'd be grown up and you wouldn't be able to stop me buying a Great Dane puppy.'

'I'm not stopping *you* buying one now,' her father said. 'Just so long as you've got the money. You come along with five hundred pounds and then . . .'

'And then what, Daddy?'

'Then we'll see.'

Four
The Show

Janie's birthday was in the early part
of January, and for a treat each year
she was always taken to London –
to the Zoo, or Madame Tussaud's, or
the Tower, or the Natural History
Museum.

'What shall we do for Janie's birthday
outing this year?' her mother said. 'Can

you think of something a bit out of
the ordinary?'

'As a matter of fact, I can,' Janie's
father said.

'What?'

'Cruft's.'

'Cruft's Dog Show?'

'Yes. Might be rather fun, don't you
think?'

'Which day? It's a four-day show, I seem
to remember.'

'Oh, the fourth day, I think.'

'Why? No, don't tell me, David; I can
read you like a book. Great Danes are
judged on the fourth day. That's it, isn't
it?'

'Well, yes. I mean, I know they're your
favourite breed, Sally.'

'Not by any chance yours too?'

'Well, yes. But I just thought it might be fun for Janie.'

'I see. Don't you think it might be a bit hard on the child? She may not be satisfied with an invisible Great Dane. It isn't as if you had any intention of buying a puppy.'

'No,' said her husband. 'Though I told Janie *she* could buy one.'

'You did *what*?'

'I said that if she came along with five hundred pounds clutched in her hot little hand, then I wouldn't stop her buying a Dane puppy.'

'You say the stupidest things sometimes. Next thing you know, she'll be robbing a bank.'

'Well, shall we go to Cruft's or shan't we?'

'Ask Janie.'

'A dog show?' Janie said when the idea was put to her. 'What dog show?'

'Cruft's. The biggest of them all. There'll probably be something like twenty thousand dogs there altogether. Of every breed.'

'Great Danes?'

'Of course.'

'Harlequin Great

Danes like Henry?'

'Sure to be some. Though they'll look a bit different from Henry.'

'Why?'

'Well, you can't see him too well.'

'Can he come to Cruft's?'

'No.'

'Poor old boy,' said Janie, fondling an invisible ear.

'I'll tell you all about it afterwards.'

*

Apart from those old snapshots of Rupert, Janie had never in her life set eyes upon a Great Dane until that unforgettable day shortly after her eighth birthday. They had walked into the great hall of Olympia and made their way past the judging of a whole lot of other breeds – terriers and collies and gun dogs and many more – and suddenly there were the giants, a ring full of them.

Black and blue, fawn and brindle and harlequin, they stood and showed themselves in all their majestic dignity.

The judge was a little woman, small enough, it seemed to Janie, to have gone for a ride on any one of the great dogs whose points she was so carefully examining.

Janie and her mother and father watched at the ringside as class succeeded class, and handlers stood their charges before the little judge, or walked or ran around the ring, the huge dogs striding out beside them. Tall men or short men, thin ladies or fat, old or young, they each had something in common, thought Janie – a Great Big Beautiful Dane. If only we could have one some day, she said to herself.

A man beside them noticed the rapt expression on Janie's face.

'Bet you wish you had a dog like one of those,' he said with a smile.

'Actually,' said Janie, 'I have. He's called Henry.'

'Imagine that!' said the friendly man.

'Henry's rather out of the ordinary,' Janie's mother said.

'Out of this world,' said her father.

They stayed and watched till the end of the judging, till the little woman had made her choice between Best Dog and Best Bitch. Both appeared equally beautiful to Janie – every one of the Danes there, it seemed to her, was faultless; she couldn't see any difference between them except colour. But she desperately wanted the dog to win Best of Breed because, just by chance, he was a harlequin. And her wish was granted.

'He's beautiful!' Janie said.

'Isn't he just!'

'They all were.'

'Weren't they just!'

Afterwards they went round the benches, and there

he was, with his rosettes and his prize cards and his proud owner.

Janie pushed between a small crowd of admirers to get a closer look. The dog, she could see, knew just what a clever fellow he was. He had a kind of smile on his great face and his long tail wagged slowly and majestically.

'He's called Champion Larkmeadow Nobleman of Merlincourt,' she told her parents.

'Gosh! What a mouthful.'

'But his owner called him Bob. I heard him.'

'That's better.'

'Funny thing though,' said Janie.

'What?'

'He looked just *exactly* like Henry.'

Five
The Tea Leaves

The postbox was at the top end of the village, not much more than a hundred yards from Janie's front gate. It was, in fact, set into the low garden wall of Mrs Garrow's cottage, and Janie sometimes wondered how the old lady posted any letters she might write. Did she come out into the lane and post them from the front like everyone else, or did she stay inside her garden and stretch over the wall, then feel for the opening in the box and post them, so to speak, upside down? No, she wouldn't be tall enough, would she?

One day she found the answer.

'Take this letter up to the post for me, Janie, will you, please?' her mother had said, and Janie set off, the letter in one hand, the lead in the other, the collar around Henry's invisible neck.

She was approaching the postbox when she saw Mrs Garrow come out of her front door, also carrying a letter, and walk across her little bit of lawn to a spot directly behind the bright red box.

She'll never be able to do it; she's too short, Janie thought, but then Mrs

Garrow seemed suddenly to rise higher,
and she leaned right over the top of the
wall and posted her letter.

Straightening up, she saw Janie and let out a burst of quacking laughter.

'Bet you thought I wasn't tall enough to do that!' she said. 'And I wouldn't be if it weren't for these,' and Janie could see that the old lady was standing on top of a little pair of wooden steps positioned behind the wall.

'I always enjoy doing that, Janie,' Mrs Garrow said. ''Specially as I always feel somehow that the postbox is mine, seeing as it's set in my wall.'

'Oh,' said Janie. 'Is it all right if I post my letter in it?'

'Course it is!' cried Mrs Garrow with another volley of quacks. 'Though I'm surprised to see *you* carrying it.'

'What d'you mean?' Janie asked.

'Well, I'd have thought that great animal of yours would be carrying it for you in his mouth. Some dogs do, you know. My! He's a size, isn't he? What's his name?'

'Henry,' said Janie.

'Well I never!' said Mrs Garrow. 'D'you know what, Janie? That was my late husband's name.'

'Oh,' said Janie. 'I'm sorry,' she added.

'No need to be sorry, dear,' said Mrs Garrow. 'He's been dead and gone these twenty years, though never a day passes when I don't think of him. And you know what? There's a lot in common between your Henry and mine.'

'How d'you mean?' Janie said.

'Well, my Henry was a great big chap too – he didn't need a stepladder to post a letter – and another thing, he was quiet, just like your dog. He doesn't bark much, does he?'

'No,' Janie said.

'Saw one just like him on the telly, couple of weeks ago,' Mrs Garrow said. 'Some big dog show it was.'

'Cruft's!' said Janie. 'We went there!'

'Did you take Henry?'

'No, but there was a dog there just exactly like him and he won the prize for Best of Breed. Another harlequin Great Dane, he was.'

'A harlequin Great Dane, eh?' said Mrs

Garrow, and she looked down from her
perch at the dangling collar and nodded.

'I see,' she said.

'And Daddy says I can have a real one –
I mean, another one – but only on one
condition.'

'And what's that?'

'I have to have five hundred pounds.'

'That's a lot of money.'

'It's a fortune!'

Mrs Garrow looked down at Janie and
her invisible dog, and her wrinkled face
creased some more, into a smile.

'Talking of fortunes, Janie,' she said,
'how would you like me to tell yours?'

'Oh, could you? Oh yes, please,' said
Janie.

'Come in and have a cup of tea then.'

'I'd better ask Mum,' said Janie.

'You do that,' said Mrs Garrow. 'I've got some nice cake.'

When Janie returned, permission granted, Mrs Garrow called from her front door, 'Come on in.'

'What about Henry?' Janie said.

'He'd better stay in the garden,' Mrs Garrow said. 'My old black cat doesn't like dogs.'

'All right,' said Janie, and she came in through the gate and dropped the collar and lead on the lawn. 'Down, Henry,' she said, and, 'Stay.'

'Now,' said Mrs Garrow when they had drunk their tea, 'let's have a look in your cup.'

For a long moment she studied the tea
leaves in the bottom of the cup, very
carefully.

Then she said, 'Janie, I think you're going to be lucky.'

'Why? What can you see?' Janie asked.

'Look,' said Mrs Garrow, handing the cup back.

Janie looked in, but all she could see was a scatter of black tea leaves at the bottom of the white cup.

'I can't see anything,' she said.

'You've got to know what you're looking for,' said Mrs Garrow. 'There's a shape there all right – a great big shape it is, no doubt about it, and what's more, it's black-and-white.'

'A harlequin Great Dane!' cried Janie. 'Is that what it is?'

Mrs Garrow smiled her crinkly smile.

'I shouldn't be surprised,' she said. 'And

now you'd best get off home.'

Out on the lawn, Janie picked up the end of the lead.

'Heel, Henry!' she said, and, 'Thank you for the tea, Mrs Garrow. I hope the tea leaves were right.'

'Talking of leaves,' said Mrs Garrow, 'this lawn's covered in them. I'd better sweep them up. Bye-bye, Janie dear.'

'Goodbye,' Janie said.

For a moment she stood in the lane by the postbox, looking over the low wall. On the lawn old Mrs Garrow was sweeping away with a long broomstick of birch twigs, watched by her black cat.

Six
The Money

'I'm bankrupt,' said Janie's mother.

'And I soon shall be,' said her father. 'I don't think it's fair. Whoever heard of a dog playing Monopoly?'

''Specially an invisible dog,' his wife said.

Janie sat grinning, a great stack of money in front of her. She patted the unseen head at her side.

'You played well,' she said.

It had been Janie's idea that Henry should take part in the game. She threw the dice for him, of course, and moved his symbol round the board, and collected the rents from all his properties as well as her own. As always, she played with the top-hat, her mother with the flat-iron and her father with the car. Henry's symbol, naturally, had to be the dog.

'OK,' said Janie's father as the car landed on Henry's Park Lane hotel. 'I've had it too. You win, Janie. You and Henry.'

'Cheer up, Daddy,' Janie said. 'I've got a nice surprise for you,' and from a wad of money she peeled off a five-hundred-pound note and held it out to him.

'What's this for?' he said.

'For my Great Dane puppy.
Remember what you said? "You come
along with five hundred pounds," you
said . . .'

'Oh, no you don't,' her father said. 'It's
got to be real money if you want a real

dog. Five hundred pounds of Monopoly money indeed – you'll be lucky!'

'I think I will be,' Janie said.

*

Later, Janie's mother said, 'I wish you hadn't done that silly thing, David.'

'What silly thing?'

'Telling Janie she could have a puppy if she had five hundred pounds. You saw the look on her face just now – she genuinely believes she's going to be lucky. It's not fair on the child – there's no way she could find that amount. Either put up the money yourself or shut up about it.'

'I just might,' Janie's father said.

'Might what? Shut up?'

'No, put up the money. Ever since Janie brought out that lead and collar, I've found myself thinking of dear old Rupert and what a super dog he was and wondering why we never replaced him.

And what with Cruft's – well, I must admit I'm getting quite keen on the idea. After all, Sally, we are the right sort of people to have a big dog – we've a sizeable house and garden, we live in the country and we can afford it.'

'You told Janie we couldn't when she first asked you.'

'Yes, I know; it's all the fault of that invisible dog of hers. The more she plays that game, the more I find I want to see an actual living, breathing, flesh-and-blood Dane on that lead.'

'A harlequin.'

'Does that matter? Surely any colour would do.'

'Not for Janie it wouldn't. And it may not be easy to find exactly what we want.'

'*We?*' said her husband. 'You go along with the idea then?'

'We'll see.'

'We will,' said Janie's father, and he grinned, slyly it seemed to his wife.

'What have you got up your sleeve?' she said.

'Not up my sleeve,' said Janie's father. 'In my pocket,' and he took something out of it.

'What's that?'

'An advertisement. I cut it out of the local paper.'

'You don't mean . . .?'

'Yes. Listen. 'Great Dane puppies for sale. Blacks, blues, one harlequin.' '

'Price?'

'Doesn't say.'

'Where?'

'Not all that far away. Extraordinary, isn't it? I had no idea there was a Great Dane breeder anywhere near here. And there's a harlequin in the litter too. What a bit of luck!'

'Janie said she'd be lucky, didn't she?'

'I know. All it needs now is for five

hundred pounds to drop out of the sky and land in Janie's lap and I shall begin to believe in witchcraft.'

At that instant they heard a loud noise outside.

'What on earth was that?' Janie's father said.

Her mother went to look out of the window.

'Oh, it's only old Mrs Garrow going down the lane,' she said. 'She has the most peculiar laugh.'

'I'll say! I thought it was a duck quacking.'

'She's chatting with Janie. And she's flapping her hand up and down. Oh no, I see what she's doing – she's patting Henry.'

'That,' said Janie's father, 'has really
made my mind up. If it's got to the stage
where Janie's playing her invisible dog
game with people like Mrs Garrow, it's
high time we got a visible one.'

'Will you tell Janie?'

'No, not yet. The harlequin pup may be sold, or it may be a bitch, or it may just be a poor specimen. We must go and see the puppies.'

'When?'

'As soon as you've taken Janie to school tomorrow morning.'

'But you'll be going to work.'

'No. I'm taking the day off. I've fixed it at the office. Urgent business.'

'David! You are a slyboots!'

The postman came just as Janie was getting ready to go to school next morning, and by the time their car reached the top end of the village his van was parked outside Mrs Garrow's cottage

while he collected the outgoing mail from
the postbox.

Mrs Garrow was chatting to him and
she waved at Janie as they went by.

'Your friend,' said Janie's mother.

'She's nice,' said Janie, waving back.

'Did you enjoy going to tea with her?'

'Yes, it was interesting.'

They drove on, while the postman got
into his van and drove away, down
towards their house.

Seven
The Kennels

Back home again, Janie's mother found her husband still sitting at the breakfast table, looking very pleased with life. He waved a letter at her.

'What's up?' his wife said. 'You look as if you've won the pools.'

'*I* haven't won anything,' Janie's father said. 'Janie has. Do you remember when

she was very small I bought some
Premium Bonds for her? Well, they've
won her some money – quite a nice sum.
Here's the letter telling me so.'

'Don't tell me it's five hundred pounds!'

'No, that would be an unbelievable coincidence after what I said about buying a Great Dane puppy.'

'How much then?'

'Two hundred.'

'It won't be enough then,' Janie's mother said.

'Enough for what?'

'Why, to buy one of those puppies. For Janie to buy one, I mean, with her own money.'

They looked at one another.

'We might have to add a bit to it,' Janie's father said.

They looked at one another again, and they smiled.

'Ring up the kennels,' Janie's mother said, 'and see if they'll keep the harlequin until we get there.'

She listened anxiously to her husband's share of the conversation.

'Good morning. I'm inquiring about the pups you advertised. Are they sold?'

'I see. But you still have the harlequin?'

. . .

'Dog or bitch?'

. . .

'Oh, good. That's the one we're interested in. Can you keep him for us?'

. . .

'Yes, I understand. We must take a chance on that. We'll be with you just as soon as we can. By the way, how much are you asking for him?'

The answer to this last question seemed to take some time, but at last Janie's father put the phone down.

'The harlequin is a dog puppy,' he said, 'and he's not sold. The woman said she couldn't guarantee to keep him for us. She's sold a couple of the others but hasn't had anyone after the harlequin yet.'

'How much?' Janie's mother said. 'She seemed to take a lot of time answering when you asked her that.'

'That's because she was giving me a long spiel about how well bred this litter is, and what the mother had won, and the fact that the father is Champion

Thingummy Nobleman of Wotsitsname —
you know, the dog that won at Cruft's.'

'So, how much?'

'Five hundred pounds.'

'I'm awfully sorry,' the breeder said when
they arrived. 'No sooner had you rung off
than someone turned up, wanting the
harlequin puppy. He's just this moment
driven off; you probably passed him on
your way here.'

Janie's parents looked at one another once more, and they sighed a joint sigh.

'There are still two blacks and a blue left,' said the breeder.

'No,' Janie's mother said, 'thanks all the same. It has to be a harlequin or nothing.'

'Leave me your address and phone number then,' said the breeder. 'I might hear of something.'

'At least Janie doesn't know anything about it,' said one to the other as they drove home again, 'so she won't be disappointed.'

'And she's got a nice surprise waiting for her when she gets back from school this afternoon.'

*

'I didn't even know I had a Premium Bond,' Janie said when they showed her the letter and the cheque. 'You never told me.'

'We don't tell you everything,' her father said.

'Two hundred pounds!' Janie said. 'Nearly enough to buy half a harlequin Great Dane puppy!'

'Has it really *got* to be a harlequin?' her mother said.

'Yes. She said so.'

'Who said so?'

'Mrs Garrow.'

'What on earth has Mrs Garrow got to do with it?'

'She saw it.'

'I don't know *what* you're talking about,' her father said.

After tea Janie took the invisible dog for a walk up the lane. As she passed Mrs Garrow's cottage, the old lady looked over the garden wall and said, 'Hullo, Janie. Better luck next time.'

I don't know what you're talking about, Janie thought.

'Ask your mum

and dad,' Mrs Garrow said, just as
though she'd read Janie's mind.

'Ask them what?'

'Where they went this morning.'

'Where did you go this morning?' Janie
asked when she got home again.

'How d'you know we went anywhere?' her father said.

'I just do.'

There was a pause.

'Tell her,' her mother said.

At that moment the phone rang. It was the Great Dane breeder.

'I've just this minute had a thought,' she said. 'Since you just missed that puppy this morning and are set on having a harlequin, I've had an idea, if you're interested. I have a nine-month-old harlequin dog that might do you. He's a good typical specimen, with a lovely nature, but he has a fault that spoils him for the show ring.'

'What sort of fault?' Janie's mother said.

'He's got a kink in his tail – a little sort

of twist near the end of it.
He was born like that, but
I've kept him on because
he's such a lovable

character. Would you like to see
him?'

They arrived once more at the kennels,
this time with Janie. The breeder looked
at her as she stood, lead in hand, collar
dangling. 'That's a biggish collar,' she said.
'Have you had a Dane before?'

'We had one called Rupert,' Janie said,
'when I was very small, but he was fawn,
not a harlequin like this one.'

'Which one?' said the breeder.

'Janie has an invisible dog,' her father
said. 'He goes everywhere with her. He's
never any trouble.'

73

'Sit, Henry!' Janie said.

'Did you say Henry?' said the breeder. 'How extraordinary! Hang on half a tick, I'll fetch the dog.'

Of course they all fell in love with him at first sight. Already he seemed enormous, with feet like soup plates. He did not squirm or wriggle as a puppy would have done, but stood steady in black-and-white dignity as befitted someone who was almost grown-up.

'His nose is partly black and partly pink!' Janie's father said as the young dog sniffed at them.

'That's all right,' the breeder said. 'A harlequin's allowed a butterfly nose.'

'And he's got one brown eye and one

blue!' said Janie's mother, as he smiled at them.

'A wall eye. That's all right too. He's a good typical specimen, with a lovely nature, but, like I said, he has a kink in his tail – that little sort of twist near the end of it.'

As if he understood, the dog slowly wagged his tail.

'I like that,' Janie said. 'I want to buy him, please.'

'*You* want to?' the breeder said, smiling. 'Have you got enough money of your own, d'you think?'

'I've got two hundred pounds,' Janie said.

'I won't charge you that much,' the breeder said. 'As I told you, he's no good for show, with that fault. But I don't think

I can give him to you – he's cost me a lot
to rear. On the other hand, I feel sure that
you'll give him a really good home. So
shall we say a hundred pounds?'

Janie put out a hand.

'It's a deal,' she said. 'What's he called?'

'You aren't going to believe it,' the
breeder said. 'In fact I must confess that
there's something very strange about all

this. But he's called Henry.'

Janie nodded. It was as though she had expected this news.

Carefully she unbuckled the collar from the invisible dog and fastened it again around the neck of his successor.

'Good boy, Henry,' she said.

Eight
The Twist

About a week later Janie came out of the
front gate and turned up the lane, the lead
in her right hand, her dog walking steadily
at heel with his long strides, his great
head not far below her shoulder. From the
buckle of his collar hung a new round
metal disc that said, above the telephone
number, HENRY.

They walked up the village until they came to Mrs Garrow's wall, with the red postbox set into it, and Janie opened the garden gate and went in. Inside the porch of the cottage were Mrs Garrow's wellies and, leaning in the corner, the long broomstick that she used for sweeping up leaves. Her cat sat on the mat.

'My old black cat doesn't like dogs,' Mrs Garrow had said, but to Janie's surprise it stood up and began to rub itself against one of Henry's long legs, purring loudly. Henry looked embarrassed.

Janie knocked on the front door, and after a moment old Mrs Garrow opened it, smiling her crinkly smile.

'Hullo,' Janie said. 'This is Henry.'

'I know that, dear,' said Mrs Garrow. 'You showed him to me before, lots of times, don't you remember?'

She patted the dog.

'Who's a good boy then?' she said. 'He's looking ever so well, Janie. You must be proud of him.'

'I am,' Janie said. 'D'you see, he's got a butterfly nose and a wall eye? There's only one thing meant to be wrong with him though I don't think it matters a bit, and that's the twist in his tail.'

'It was all in the tea-leaves,' Mrs Garrow said.

'I don't understand,' Janie said. 'How can you know these things?'

Mrs Garrow let out her usual volley of quacks.

'Aha, Janie my dear!' she said. 'That's the twist in the tale.'

Read on for an extract from

The
QUEEN'S NOSE

by Dick King-Smith

One
Uncle Ginger

Harmony and Rex Ruff Monty sat side by side in the old chicken house at the bottom of the garden.

No chickens had lived there for many years — Mr and Mrs Parker did not like animals — but a vague sour smell of the birds lingered on. There was still some fusty straw in the nest boxes, and the perches were barnacled with old dry droppings.

The place was small, and dark, for there was

only one little wire-netting window, with a wooden shutter which you could slide across if the rain blew in; the door was low, so that a grown-up person would have found it hard to enter; and, except the perches, there was nothing to sit on but an upturned tea chest.

None of this mattered to Harmony, for the chicken house was her retreat. Here she came to be alone, which she mostly liked to be. Not of course that she was ever quite alone. There was always Rex Ruff Monty.

Harmony Parker was a girl of ten. She had very large brown eyes. She looked as though she wouldn't say 'Boo!' to a goose. This was true in one sense, for she wouldn't have said anything so silly. A goose was one of the dozens of different creatures she dreamed about owning, as she sat on her tea chest. Harmony longed to have an animal of her own.

'I wish I could,' she said to Rex Ruff Monty. 'As well as you, I mean.'

Rex Ruff Monty was a dog of fifty-nine. He

had only one eye, the other had dropped out. He
had first belonged to Harmony's grandmother
and had originally been a rich chocolate colour
and quite hairy. Now he was grey and bald all
over. He was recognizably some sort of large
terrier, an Airedale perhaps. Three of his legs
were still quite stiff but the fourth, the right
foreleg, was squidgy and elongated and even
more hairless than the rest of him. It was by this
leg that Harmony always carried him.

'Why do they have to be so mean?' she said.

She picked up Rex Ruff Monty, who was standing on the tea chest awkwardly, tipped over on his soft leg with his blind side towards her, and turned him round.

'You tell me,' she said, staring earnestly into his eye, 'why they have to be so stupid about the whole thing. It isn't as though I wanted an elephant. Or half a dozen chimpanzees. Or a troupe of liberty horses. I mean, I wouldn't mind all those but I'll settle for a pair of mice or just a gerbil. But they won't let me and you know why, don't you?'

Harmony waited, for ten seconds perhaps, as you would when having a telephone conversation, and then continued.

'Exactly. You're absolutely right, Rex Ruff Monty. Mummy thinks animals are dirty, and carry diseases.'

There was another pause.

'Who? Oh, Daddy. Well, he's just not interested. Doesn't like animals. I'm not even sure he likes people much.'

Pause.

'Except her, of course, you're right, I forgot about Simple Sissie.' Simple Sissie was Harmony's elder sister, Melody. She was fourteen and supposedly her father's favourite. She thought a great deal about her hair and her clothes. She referred to Rex Ruff Monty as 'that filthy beast', and called his owner Harm.

'So what can I do?

'Just keep on wishing, you say? Wishing will make it so, you say? Oh, Rex Ruff Monty, I *wish* it was as easy as that,' and Harmony picked him up by his soft leg, and undid the catch of the chicken-house door.

She walked slowly up the orchard, swinging Rex Ruff Monty gently from side to side. There had been a summer shower and the long grass was wet. It felt pleasantly cool against her legs and on her bare feet, like paddling in the sea. Suddenly she dived behind an apple tree and lay flat, one hand pressed over the old dog's black woollen mouth, as her sister came out through the french windows and called her name.

'Harm!' cried Melody in her usual bossy voice. 'Where are you? Mummy wants you.'

Harmony burrowed lower.

'Not a sound, Rex Ruff Monty,' she whispered. 'Wait till you see the whites of her eyes.'

She listened with pleasure to the repeated calling, and then to another voice, her mother's.

'Run down and fetch her, Melody darling. I know she's somewhere in the garden.'

'Oh Mummy, the grass is soaking! And I've got my new shoes on.'

'Hurry up, darling.'

'Oh Mummy!'

Picking her feet up high, Melody moved reluctantly into the wet jungle of the orchard. In the depths of the jungle the tigress crouched, grinning with anticipation.

'Harm!' cried Melody once more. 'Where are you? Oh come on, you little beast!'

At this invitation the tigress charged.

Two very different sounds came to the ears of the three people who sat in the room behind the french windows.

The first was a kind of horrid, throaty, grunting, bubbling, coughing roar, not very deep in tone to be sure but of a ferocity that was heart-stopping. And the second was a very loud scream.

'Oh, my nerves won't stand it!' cried Mrs Parker, levering her plump self out of her armchair. 'What on earth was that?'

Her husband placed the tips of his fingers together and looked carefully at them over his half-glasses.

'I fear,' he said acidly, 'that you have sent poor Melody into an ambush. Such a vivid imitation of the sound of a wild animal can only have been the work of your younger daughter.' (Mr Parker always referred to Harmony thus.) He looked over his fingertips at the man sitting opposite.

'I imagine,' he said, 'that you, Ginger, with your encyclopaedic knowledge of brute beasts,

may actually have recognized the sound?'

'Bengal tiger,' said the other without hesitation. 'Heard one only last month, up at Bud Bud, just before I came on leave. Didn't know there were any in Wimbledon.'

At this moment two figures burst in from the garden. One, the man called Ginger could see, was fair-haired, with very large brown eyes and an expression of angelic innocence. The other, larger and darker, had obviously just taken a nasty tumble. Her rather frilly summer frock was damp and rumpled and marked with grass stains.

'Melody darling!' cried Mrs Parker. 'Whatever . . . ?'

The victim of the ambush was torn between bursting into tears of rage or attacking her younger sister. Disliking the first alternative as too babyish and dismissing the second as too dangerous (for Harmony was a gutter fighter, no holds barred), she fled the room, her mother in anxious attendance.

'Harmony,' said Mr Parker in a weary voice, 'this is my brother and therefore your uncle, home on leave from India. I think he has never met you. At this moment I can only consider him fortunate. Now, if you will excuse me . . .' He rose and moved heavily out of the room.

'I'm Harmony,' said Harmony. She put out a rather dirty hand. The man stood up and shook it with a very large one.

'My name's Henry,' he said, 'but everybody calls me Ginger.' They looked at each other with interest.

One saw a small girl, bare-legged, dressed in a pair of old jeans that had been hacked off at the knees and a faded T-shirt which advised him to 'Save the Whale'. Her feet were not clean, and she smelt faintly of chickens.

The other unhesitatingly saw an animal.

Long ago, Harmony had firmly decided that, with a few exceptions, animals were nicer than humans. People that she knew or met she therefore saw in her mind with the ease of long practice as this or that mammal or bird or fish, even as an insect (her teacher was a female Praying Mantis).

She drew well, and expressed this fancy by portraits where the head of the person surmounted the body of the chosen animal. Locked away in her bedroom was a large scrapbook on the first page of which strutted a tubby fussy Pouter Pigeon bearing above its proud throat her mother's neat and rather vacant face. Overleaf, large, sleek and moustached, the eyes prominent beneath the bald crown, sat her father the Sea Lion. Opposite Melody, her blue eyes only the merest fraction crossed, admired her Siamese reflection in a tall looking-glass; not a hair was out of place on her glossy coat, and her long tail curled elegantly round her neat feet.

Now, looking at Uncle Ginger, bulky and tweedy, those large hands hanging loosely at the end of very long arms, Harmony instantly recognized a bear. And not just any bear. For though the colour that had given him his nickname still held good in beard and moustache, the plentiful hair of his head was speckled with early grey. A Silvertip Grizzly!

They both spoke at once.

'You're not much like Daddy,' said Harmony and 'You're not much like your sister,' said the Silvertip, and they laughed comfortably together.

'Would you like to see the garden?' Harmony

said. 'I'll show you my den.'

'Tiger's den?'

'Oh. You knew what I was pretending to be? Of course you would if you've spent a long time in India. Though there aren't many left, I believe.'

'Not many.'

'Have you ever seen one? In the jungle, I mean?'

'Yes, quite a few. And it was a very good imitation. How did you know the kind of noise an angry tiger makes?'

'Oh, films on the telly. And I've heard them at the zoo. Not angry, but hungry. And homesick, I expect.'

'You don't like zoos?'

'I'm not sure. I know the good things about them. I just feel all animals ought to be happy and you can't be happy unless you're free.'

They reached the chicken house. The Silvertip Grizzly bent himself double to get through the door, was politely offered the tea chest, and sat

down on it, head bowed under the low roof, long arms dangling. He looked at Harmony balanced on a perch.

'You're pretty keen on animals, are you?' he said.

'Yes. I like animals more than . . .'

'More than what?'

'More than most things.'

'What have you got?'

'Animals, you mean?'

'Yes.'

There was a pause.

'None,' said Harmony.

Uncle Ginger raised his head rather sharply at this and hit it on the chicken-house roof.

'No dog?' he said. 'No cat? No rabbits, guinea pigs, mice, budgies, nothing?'

Harmony shook her head. She scuffed at the floor with a bare big toe, making large capital letters in the powdery mixture of old sawdust that covered it. Uncle Ginger, sitting opposite, read the word upside down. It said:

DIRTY

'That's what Mummy and Daddy think animals are,' said Harmony in a flat voice. 'The only way I'm ever going to own an animal, any animal, is by some sort of magic. D'you believe in magic, Uncle Ginger?'

'Yes. I do.'

'They have lots of magic in India, don't they? Rope tricks and snake charmers and people lying on beds of nails and stuff?'

'Yes.'

'D'you know anything about magic? Yourself?'

'A bit.'

'Gosh! I *wish* you could use some of it while you're here. By the way, how long are you here for?'

'Couple of weeks.'

They looked at each other.

'No,' said Uncle Ginger, smiling through his beard, 'I'm not just going to go to your parents and say, "Harmony ought to have a puppy or a rabbit or something." That's between you and them. But I might be able to help.'

'Oh, I *wish* you would!'

They made their way out of the chicken house, and Uncle Ginger stretched himself. He looked up at the blue sky and then down at the brown eyes watching him. 'D'you do a lot of wishing, Harmony?' he said.

'Yes,' said Harmony. She pulled Rex Ruff Monty's tatty ears.

From the top of the garden they heard voices calling.

'Ginger!' barked the Sea Lion. 'There's a cup of tea ready.'

And 'Harmony!' cooed the Pouter Pigeon. 'Come and get tidy.'

The Siamese Cat was sulking and made no sound.

'Wishes do come true, don't they?' said Harmony in a small voice. 'Sometimes?'

The Silvertip Grizzly put a big paw on her shoulder and nodded his head.

'Sometimes,' he said.

Dick King-Smith

Born: Bitton, Gloucestershire
27 March 1922
Jobs: Soldier, farmer, salesman, teacher,
TV presenter and author

When did you start writing?
Started my first book for children, *The Fox Busters*, in 1976, got it published in 1978.
Since then I have written so many books that I think I have rather lost count!

Where do you get the ideas for your stories?
Things I've done, people I've met or known, animals I've owned or know, but mostly
it's just a question of sitting and thinking.

What are your hobbies?
Writing books for children. Sitting in the garden on summer evenings with a nice
drink. Talking to my dogs. Washing up. You'll never catch me buying a dishwasher; it
would take all the fun out of it!

Will you give your three top tips on becoming an author?
- Read as widely as you can. Try not to read rubbish, but soak up all sorts of good
  stories.
- Practise. No good saying, 'I'm going to be a writer'. Get on with it. Write about
  whatever you fancy.
- Show what you've done to someone whose opinion you respect – Mum, Dad,
  your teacher. Listen to their comments: don't get upset by them, think about them.

**And finally, if you hadn't been a writer, what do you think you
would have been?**
A farmer still. I'm glad I'm not now, I'm too blooming old to be humping sacks of
corn or pitching bales; and I shouldn't like to go back to milking cows. I wish I still
had some pigs though…

Bright and shiny
and sizzling
with fun stuff . . .

puffin.co.uk

WEB FUN

UNIQUE and exclusive digital content!
Podcasts, photos, Q&A, Day in the Life of, interviews
and much more, from Eoin Colfer, Cathy Cassidy,
Allan Ahlberg and Meg Rosoff to Lynley Dodd!

WEB NEWS

The **Puffin Blog** is packed with posts and photos from
Puffin HQ and special guest bloggers. You can also sign up
to our monthly newsletter **Puffin Beak Speak**

WEB CHAT

Discover something new EVERY month –
books, competitions and treats galore

WEBBED FEET

(Puffins have funny little feet and
brightly coloured beaks)

Point your mouse our way today!

It all started with a Scarecrow.

Puffin is seventy years old.
Sounds ancient, doesn't it? But Puffin has never been
so lively. We're always on the lookout for the next big
idea, which is how it began all those years ago.

Penguin Books was a big idea from the mind of
a man called Allen Lane, who in 1935 invented
the quality paperback and changed the world.
**And from great Penguins, great Puffins grew,
changing the face of children's books forever.**

Puffin

The first four Puffin Picture Books were hatched in 1940 and the
first Puffin story book featured a man with broomstick arms called
Worzel Gummidge. In 1967 Kaye Webb, Puffin Editor, started the
Puffin Club, promising to **'make children into readers'**.
She kept that promise and over 200,000 children became
devoted Puffineers through their quarterly instalments of
Puffin Post, which is now back for a new generation.

Puffin

Many years from now, we hope you'll look back and
remember Puffin with a smile. **No matter what your age
or what you're into, there's a Puffin for everyone.**
The possibilities are endless, but one thing is for sure:
whether it's a picture book or a paperback, a sticker book
or a hardback, **if it's got that little Puffin
on it – it's bound to be good.**